Igiiwe maamakaandemiziiwad gitaaziimag, Bill dash Doris Wilson, awenenag gaa gikino'amaa'igoowan ji zhaagi'igooyan ji ozhibii'igeyan, dash ge Sadie Debassige, awenen gaa zaagi'id de ji nimaajaayan. Owe mazina'igan gaawin daa gishkitjigaadesinonn ayaasiiyan zaagi'idiwin dash baapiyin igiwe nish niigozisan, Brandan dash Phoenix. Dash ge akina LGBQT+ abinoojiinhwag dash ge wiinawaa o'indewisiwinan, giin gaawin nazhibewizi.

For my wonderful parents, Bill and Doris Wilson, who taught me the love of writing, and for Sadie Debassige, who loved me enough to let me go. This book would not be possible without the love and laughter from my two sons, Brandan and Phoenix. And to all LGBQT+ children and their families, you are not alone.

—M.W.T.

O'owe Mazina'igan inedaamoowaa niin niwiijiiwaagan, niwiikiwenh Brandan, dash nimishoomis, Bill, awenen gaa onjid bakaan mewizha-izhi-bimaadiziwin odaanang apane zaagi' dash ge gii odaapinig. Owe akina abinoojiiwag miziwe gaa ayaawad awenen gaawin gaa ayaasiwad zaagiyin dash ge bami'iyaasiwad wiinawaa inodewisiwinan dash ge awe'ego'. Giin gii nitaawigi gowek.

This book is dedicated to my best friend, my brother Brandan, and to my grandad, Bill, who even though he came from a different era always loved and accepted me. This is for every child out there who doesn't have the love and support from their families and peers. You were born this way.

—P.W.

A Note on the Translation: There are two names for the term Two Spirit used in this book, Niizh Manidoowag and Nizho-jiibayid, representing the distinct Anishinaabemowin dialects of the authors and of the translator.

Library and Archives Canada Cataloguing in Publication

Title: Phoenix ani' gichichi-i' / gaa ozhibii'ang Marty Wilson-Trudeau wiiji Phoenix Wilson ; gaa
   waawiindan-mazinaakizoige i' Megan Kyak-Monteith ; gaa aanikanootaamaaget Kelvin Morrison =
   Phoenix gets greater / written by Marty Wilson-Trudeau with Phoenix Wilson ; illustrated by
   Megan Kyak-Monteith ; translated by Kelvin Morrison.
Other titles: Phoenix gets greater
Names: Wilson-Trudeau, Marty, author. | Wilson, Phoenix, author. | Kyak-Monteith, Megan,
   illustrator. | Morrison, Kelvin, translator. | Container of (work): Wilson-Trudeau, Marty.
   Phoenix gets greater. | Container of (expression): Wilson-Trudeau, Marty. Phoenix gets greater.
   Ojibwa.
Description: Text in Anishinaabemowin-Ojibwe translation and in original English.
Identifiers: Canadiana (print) 20220479402 | Canadiana (ebook) 20220479437 | ISBN 9781772603248 (hardcover) | ISBN
   9781772603255 (EPUB) | ISBN 9781772603330 (Kindle)
Subjects: LCSH: Two-spirit people—Juvenile fiction. | LCGFT: Picture books. | LCGFT: Fiction.
Classification: LCC PS8645.I4748 P46165 2023 | DDC jC813/.6—dc23

*Second Story Press gratefully acknowledges the support of the Ontario Arts Council and the Canada Council for the Arts for our
publishing program. We acknowledge the financial support of the Government of Canada through the Canada Book Fund.*

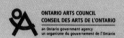

Published by
Second Story Press
20 Maud Street, Suite 401
Toronto, Ontario, Canada
M5V 2M5
www.secondstorypress.ca

"*Phoenix Gets Greater* is a timely and necessary addition to our collective Two-Spirit stories! Its collaboration
between mother and son, its engrossing color palettes that reflect Anishinaabe acceptance and wholeness,
and its charming, swirling protagonist make for a story that should be shared with all of our children.
Broaching the vast topic of Two-Spirit identities, Marty Wilson-Trudeau and Phoenix Wilson have made a
book I wish I had when I was a kid—the wonders this book will do for our Indigenous and/or queer youth!"

—Joshua Whitehead, award-winning author of *Jonny Appleseed*

Phoenix Ani' Gichichi-I'

Phoenix Gets Greater

gaa ozhibii'ang / written by
Marty Wilson-Trudeau *wiiji/with* **Phoenix Wilson**

gaa waawiindan-mazinaakizoige i' / illustrated by
Megan Kyak-Monteith

gaa aanikanootaamaaget / translated by
Kelvin Morrison

Second Story Press

Apii Phoenix gii nitaawigid, wiin gii agwonaawi'apiiji biisaanikweweni. Osayenyan ogii izhin kaanaan 'Miishaa' izhi-wiinimaan miishaa onji wiin gii miishizi digo makwa! Phoenix's Omaamaayin dash osayenyan apiiji ogii zhawenimigoon.

————

When Phoenix was born, he was covered in very fine hair. His big brother called him 'Fuzzy' because he was fuzzy like a bear! Phoenix's mom and brother loved him very much.

Aanawi Phoenix gii aakozi, dash wiin mashkikiiwininiwag gii windamaagoon gaawin wiikaa daa gaagiigidosii, daa baambisii maagiwebizigan, gemaa daa basikawaadang bikwaakwad.

Phoenix's omaamaayin ogii nookwezigoon aniye niiwin mashkikiiwan: bashkodwijiibik, giishkaandag, dash ge wiingashk. Ogii gaganoonaan Gizhiwe-manidoo andaso-giizhig megwaa Phoenix apii gii ayaad aakoziiwigamig.

————————

But Phoenix was sick, and his doctors said he would never be able to talk, ride a bike, or kick a ball.

Phoenix's mom smudged him with the four medicines: sage, tobacco, cedar, and sweetgrass. She talked to the Creator every day while Phoenix was in the hospital.

Bekaago', Phoenix gii ani minomajiyo'! Gii
bi giiwe zigo apii Waasiingwaagani-giizhig
dash gii wawezhi'o babiiwaawan okoosimaan
biidoshkigan.

———————

Slowly, Phoenix felt better!

He came home just in time for Halloween and dressed up in a tiny
pumpkin costume.

Phoenix ogii mikaan omaamaayins oginiiwaande, biiswewaaboowan dash ogii baamiitoon miziwe gii bi baa iyaad. Gii ditibineyizoni dash gii bi baa odaabaadan giiwitaa-ayi'ii waakaa'iganing gabegiizhig.

I'idi odaminowigamig. Phoenix gii minwendan ji ganwaabaamad odaminwaaganag akina ayaawad onishishin, odisiwinan bagwaaniganan. Wiin gii onaabandanan gaa nookaa'iyaag, nookijiiyaagin odaminiwaaganag, izhiwan odaminiwaaganan, dash ge odaminiwaaganan gaa gagaanwanikwewad. Wiibago' gii giiwed, gii gashkiiweginan gizingwe'on otigwaan dash gii nindi-kaazo ji ayaad gagaanwankiwewinan gewiin, gii igizhibaabinwebinaataagood.

—————

Phoenix found his mom's pink, fluffy blanket and took it with him everywhere. He rolled in it and dragged it around the house all day.

At the toy store, Phoenix loved to look at the dolls with all the pretty, colorful fabrics.

He picked out soft, squishy dolls, fashion dolls, and dolls with long hair. As soon as he got home, he wrapped a towel on his head and pretended he had long hair too, swishing it all around.

Phoenix gii gikendaaso ji gizhibaabizod, igizhibaabinwebiaataagood, dash gizhibaabini'od aapiji ge wiins niimi gikinoo'amagewikwewan ge gichi-inendamo!

Imaa niimi'idiwinan, Phoenix gii gizhibaase, gii gizhibaase, dash iwe miskogaadagan wiins mashkosiwan-bwaanzhiiwi'on gii gizhibaaseni ge.

Aanawi Phoenix zhawendan agwinaan niimi'idin maawach-babenak. Wiin gii atoon biise waaboowan odiniimaaganan, dash gii niimi dibishkoo miikwaadizi memegwaa.

————

Phoenix learned to spin, swish, and swirl so well even his ballet teacher was impressed!

At Pow Wows, Phoenix twirled and twirled, and the wool on his grass dance regalia twirled with him.

But Phoenix loved shawl dancing best. He put his fluffy blanket on his shoulders, went up on his tiptoes, and danced like a beautiful butterfly.

Phoenix gaawin ogii ayaawaasiin niijiiwag gaa minwendamowad bimaakoweba'igaadegin, bimaawadaasoowidaabaanan, dash ge ikowebinan-aki-wiiyasenh-daabaanan. Wiin gii niijiiwan ingiweg awenen gaa minwenimag odaminwaaganag dash gaa niimiwad ge.

Aanawi gooding, aanind abinoojiiwag gii miikinjiyaan Phoenix onji wiin naawaaj gii nimweniman odaminwaaganan dash inwe bimaawadaasoowidaabaanan. Wiinawaa gii inenimigoon mayagizi onji wiin gaawin gii izhichigesii dibishko igiwe aanind gwiiwizensag wiinawaa e-gikinoo'amaagesaadjigan.

————————

Phoenix didn't have friends who liked hockey, trucks, and bulldozers. He made friends with those who liked dolls and dancing too.

But sometimes, other kids made fun of Phoenix because he preferred dolls to trucks. They thought he was strange because he didn't act like the rest of the boys in their class.

"Aapiji niibiwa zoongide'ewin giinigo ji ayaayin dash ji naanaadamoowag aanind aweyag," omaamaawin gii windamowan Phoenix.

Wiin osayenyansan gii gagwe ganawenimigoon gikinoo'amaadiiwigamig, dash Phoenix gewaabi' gii maanedam.

"It takes a lot of courage to be yourself and stand up to others," his mom told Phoenix.

His brother tried to protect him at school, but Phoenix still felt sad.

Goding gizheb, wiin gii wiiji nabadabi omaamaayin dash osayenyan. Mawid, ogii wiindamowan, "Niin dayekoz gaazowaan weniin niin. Gaawin niin diziyaasii gowek aanind gwiiwizens ayaawad niye-giknoo'amaagesaad. Niin bakaan dizhi'iyaayin. Niin igo nibakaanis."

Phoenix ogii wiindamoowan Ningodoodeman wiin manidoowe'i. "Niin bagosedan giinawaa gaawin ji ishkwaa zaagi'igoowan, dash giinawaa ji adaapinamaageyin awenen niin."

———————

One day, he sat down with his mom and brother. Crying, he told them, "I'm tired of hiding who I am. I'm not like the other boys in my class. I feel different. I am different."

Phoenix told his family he was gay. "I hope you won't stop loving me, and you'll accept me for who I am."

Phoenix's omaamaayin dash osayeyan gii wiikobinan besho dash gii maaji maweyok ge.

"Niinayend gaawiin wiikaan gaa ishkwaa zaagi'igoowin," Phoenix's maamaawin gii ikido. "Niinayend gi zaagi'igo wenen giin, dash mii'I giin gi nitaa niinayend minawaanigomin, Niin apiji gichi-apiitenimin."

"Gaawin gegoo azhiyaasinoon ji bakaaniziyin," osayayensan minoyeyad. "Miiyedigo di giin ji minawaanigwendaman."

––––––––––

Phoenix's mom and brother pulled him close and started to cry too.

"We'll never stop loving you," Phoenix's mom said. "We love exactly who you are, and for that, you make us happy. I'm so proud of you."

"There's nothing wrong with being different," his brother comforted. "All that matters is that you're happy."

"Giinayend akina gi mii'idoomin jiibay biinji'iye'iimin," Phoenix's maamamyin waawindan. "Gi miinigoomin bimaadiziwin dash babaamiwizhigoomin. Aanawi giinayend Anishinaabe izhitwaawin ayaawag Niizho jiibay ayaa'ag, Niizh Manidoowag, wenwen ayaawad majinizh ikwezens dash ge gwiiwizens jiibage. Niizh giinayind ikidowin iwe Niizh dash ge manidoowag ganage jiibay.

————

"We all carry a spirit within us," Phoenix's mom explained. "It gives us life and guides us. But in our Anishinaabe culture there are Two Spirit people, Niizh Manidoowag, who have both girl and boy spirits. Niizh is our word for two and manidoowag means spirit.

"A'aw ozhi igooyin apiji gichi apiitendaagos' onji giin gidinendam dash ginamaji' minjinizhi gwiiwizensag dash ikwezensag. Anishinaabe oodenaaning gii ayaanaanaawan gichi minwaadendamowin igiiwe Niizh Manidoowag. Wiinawaas Nibwaakaawin, noojimo'iwewinan, dash gii'igoshimonan gii wiiji'iyaagin giinayend oodenaaning, dash wiinawaa gii zhawendiwag ji niimiwad dash gizhibaabizewad—daabishkoo giin iyaayin."

———————

"That makes you extra special because you think and feel like both boys and girls. Anishinaabe communities have great respect for Niizh Manidoowag. Their wisdom, healing ways, and visions help our communities, and they love to dance and twirl— just like you."

Phoenix gii maajii zhoomiingweni. Gaawin wiin gii debwetaasiin. Ayaawag aanind awiyag awenen daabishkoo wiin ayaayid! Dash Niizh Manidoowag oobimiidoon apiitendaagwad onagiminiwan wiin Anishinnabe izhitwaawin, ge.

Ge-giizhig, wiin gii odaminwaadan odaminwaaganag dash gii baapi gii madwese dash ge gizhibaabizod wiin oginiiwaanzowin, biiswe waabiiwan. I'gwe aanind abinoojiiwag ikidowinan gaawin apiji gii wiisagendami'sinoon geyaadi onji Phoenix gii apiitenimozi gii Nizho-jiibayid.

Noongom, Phoenix odaawanan wiijiiwaginag awenen gaa odaapinamaagewad awenen wiin ayaayid.

Phoenix started to smile. He couldn't believe it. There were other people who were just like him! And Niizh Manidoowag carried an important role in his Anishinaabe culture, too.

The next day, he played with his dolls and laughed as he swished and swirled in his pink, fluffy blanket. The other kids' words didn't hurt so much anymore because Phoenix was proud of being Two Spirit.

Now, Phoenix has friends who accept him for all of who he is.

Geyaabi wiin mashkosiw dash agwinaan niimi'idiwinan—wiin madwese'l dash ge gizhibaabizo'i megwaa wiin osayenyan dash ge omaamaayin moojigendamowag dash bapasininjii'odizowag!

He still dances grass and shawl at Pow Wows—he twirls and swishes and swirls while his brother and mom cheer and clap!

Marty Wilson-Trudeau awe Anishinaabe-kwe ozhibii-igeyi onjiyaa M'Chigeeng, Ontario, dash ge Gikinawaaji-iwewin gekinoo'amaaged imaa St. Charles College imaa Sudbury, Ontario. Wiin Maamaayi niish maamakaandemiziiwad ogozisan, Brandan dash Phoenix Wilson.

Marty Wilson-Trudeau is an Anishinaabe Kwe writer originally from M'Chigeeng, Ontario, and a drama teacher at St. Charles College in Sudbury, Ontario. She is a mother to two wonderful sons, Brandan and Phoenix Wilson.

Phoenix Wilson Anishinaabe waabanda'iwe-I' dash niimid dash gichi apiitenimo-izi. Phoenix gii maaji niimi ballet gii niso-biboonend, mashkosiw-niimi'idiwin gii naano-biboonend, dash waabanda-iwe-I' gii ongodawaaso-biboonend. Wiin daa waabandaa-izi' dibishkoo-iniwe anokaajiganan *Longmire*, *Letterkenny*, dash ge apiji apiidedaagod mazinaateseyin *Wild Indian*. Phoenix noomaye' na'iiwin midaaswi-ashi-bezig aandi wiin gii apiidendaamo akinaa e-gikinoo'ammgesadinoon dash onjidaawin ji gizhikood ji aanikoominozhijige'inan dibaakonigewinini.

Phoenix Wilson is an Anishinaabe actor and dancer and is very proud of who he is. Phoenix started dancing ballet at age three, grass dancing at age five, and acting at age six. He can be seen in such projects as *Longmire*, *Letterkenny*, and the critically acclaimed movie *Wild Indian*. Phoenix is currently in Grade 11 where he excels in all his classes and has ambitions of becoming a corporate lawyer.

Megan Kyak-Monteith, onjii Pond Inlet, Nunavut, wiin Inuk gikinoo'amaage dash aage dash aage dash zhizhoobii'igeyi'. Ji-zhaabishkaayid imaa NSCAD Gabe-gikendaasoowigamig 2019, wiin noongom abi' dash anokii Halifax, Nova Scotia. Wiin waabadaa'inan anokaajiganan. Wiin anokii nawaaj moozhag iniwe Anishinaabe dibaajimowinan.

Megan Kyak-Monteith, from Pond Inlet, Nunavut, is an Inuk illustrator and painter. Graduating from NSCAD University in 2019, she currently lives and works in Halifax, Nova Scotia. In her illustrative projects, she works most often with Indigenous stories.

Kiitaabines onji Nigigoonsiminikaaning omaa Northwestern Ontario, Washashk o'dodem. Anokii Anishinaabemowin Aanikanoojiiyen imaa Niizhwaaching Aanikoobiijigeng Gikinoo'amaadiiwigamig, aanikanootang mazina'iganan, mazinaatesijiganan, dash ge dibaajimowinesan, mii ige iniwe aanikanootang Gichi-ayaa'aag dibaajimwinan dash baakan-aanind ozhijiganan ji aabajijigaadegin aabinoojiwigamingoonan, Gikinoo'amaadiiwigamingoonan dash ge oodenaawinan. Wiin o'minwedam o'danaakiiwan, awe aakina aweya ji gikedamowad, nisitamowad dash aaniin gowek enitaagod inwewin. E'ye ge anokii dibendaagozi gaa ganedamowad gikendamowinan anokaajigan gaa miigiwewad Fort Frances Rainy River School Board dash ge maada'ookii dibaajimowinan, gikendamowin inaadiziwinan, Anishinaabe gikinoo'amaadiiwigamigoon inaapinewinan dash ge gigikwe'inan akiikaaning.

Kelvin Morrison (Kiitaabines) is from Nigigoonsiminikaaning First Nation in Northwestern Ontario, Wazhashk (muskrat) clan. He works as an Anishinaabemowin translator at Seven Generations Education Institute, translating books, videos, and short stories, as well as Elders' stories and resource materials for daycares, schools, and communities. He enjoys creating tools so all can learn, understand, and hear how Anishinaabemowin sounds. He also works in the Knowledge Keepers Program offered by the Fort Frances Rainy River School Board, sharing stories, cultural knowledge, residential school experience, and teachings about the Land.